Oliver Moon and the Potion Commotion

Sue Mongredien

Illustrated by
Jan McCafferty

USBORNE

For Tom Powell, with lots of love

from Mum x

First published in 2006 by Usborne Publishing Ltd., Usborne House, 83-85 Saffron Hill, London EC1N 8RT, England. www.usborne.com

Text copyright © Sue Mongredien, 2006
Illustration copyright © Usborne Publishing Ltd., 2006

A CIP catalogue record for this book is available from the British Library.

JFMAMJJ SOND/08

ISBN 9780746073063

Printed in Great Britain.

Contents

Chapter
One

Oliver Moon was the hardest working junior wizard at Magic School.

He was smashing at Spellcraft.

He was tip-top at Toad Training.

And as for his broomstick flying...it was absolutely brilliant!

"One of our most promising pupils," Mrs. MacLizard, the head teacher, had written in his last school report. "If he could just perfect his potion brewing, he'd be dynamite."

But potion brewing wasn't Oliver's biggest problem. Oh, no. His biggest problems were at home. One problem was his mum. The other problem was his dad. And actually, the Witch Baby was a bit of a problem, too.

Oliver knew his mum and dad weren't the worst witch and wizard in the world. Not quite.

They hadn't "Gone Good" like Hattie Toadtrumper's mum and dad.

They weren't knee-knockingly scary like Boris Batbottom's mum and dad.

And they definitely weren't super-strict like poor old Pippi Prowlcat's parents.

The Moon Family

No, Oliver's mum and dad were just eye-poppingly awful at *being a witch and wizard*. They didn't have a clue. It was very embarrassing.

"I can't be bothered to cook in that cauldron any more," his dad said one day. He'd burned the scorpion stew again the evening before, and the kitchen was *still* full of curling black smoke. "I've bought us this microwave instead. You can steam a slug in thirty seconds. Look at that beauty go!"

"But Dad, you can't stir spells in a microwave," Oliver pointed out.

His dad wasn't listening. He was too busy poaching prickleberries to go with his slug.

PING! went the microwave.

"Ping!" echoed the Witch Baby, stretching out a fat hand for a taste.

"Yum," slurped Mr. Moon, licking his lips.

The next day, Oliver's mum said,
"I'm not wearing that pointy hat
any more. I've just had my
hair done and I don't
want it going flat."
"But Mum, pointy
hats heat up the magic
in your brain," Oliver
reminded her. "You can't cast spells with
a cold head!"

His mum didn't pay any attention.
She was too busy brushing her hair with
her thornspike brush.

SQUIRT! went the hairspray.

"Poo!" squeaked the Witch Baby,
wrinkling her nose.

"Gorgeous," said Mrs. Moon, winking
at herself in the mirror.

And there was worse to come...

"Mum and I have had enough of wearing dusty old cloaks," Dad announced. "We want to wear trendy clothes for a change."

Oliver *almost* told his dad that purple pantaloons and glittery gold tank tops were not trendy at all, but he didn't want to hurt his feelings. Instead, he reminded him that a swishable cloak was a key part of the wizarding wardrobe. "You need to swish before you can wish, Dad," he said. "Remember?"

Mr. Moon didn't change his mind. He was too busy ironing his orange vest.

SSSSS! went the iron.

"Yuck!" yelped the Witch Baby, blinking at the brightness.

"Perfect!" cried Mr. Moon, doing a twirl. "Swishing is for squares."

As for broomsticks...Oliver didn't even want to *think* about broomsticks. His mum and dad had flatly refused to put their bottoms anywhere near one ever since his mum's nasty accident with the tanglebranch tree.

"But broomstick flying is what we *do*," Oliver begged them. "You can't be a witch or wizard without swooping through the night sky."

"It's too dangerous," his mum said, shuddering. "I might crash again."

"It's too cold," his dad said, shivering.

"I might catch something. You know me and my coughs."

"Atchoo!" sneezed the Witch Baby, wiping her nose on her sleeve.

Oliver glared at her.

"Anyway, we've got a car now," his mum and dad said together. "*And* it's got a stereo. You can't listen to music on a broomstick, can you?"

"I give up," Oliver said to his best friend, Jake Frogfreckle, as they walked to school one Monday. "Mum and Dad are so unmagical, it's not true. And they're just getting worse."

"Maybe they'll grow out of it," Jake said helpfully.

Oliver snorted. "Grow out of it? When?

Mum's two hundred and four years old already. Dad is two hundred and twenty next month. You'd think they'd act their ages by now." He shook his head. "No, they're never going to change. Never in a billion years!"

Chapter
Two

Monday was usually Oliver's favourite
day of the week. Today, though, nothing
seemed to be going right.

First of all, he muddled up his
Transforma spell in Magic Class. Instead
of turning Jake into a sausage sandwich,
he turned Mr. Goosepimple into a
donkey.

"Hee-haw!" brayed Mr. Goosepimple, stamping his hoof crossly.

"Oops," said Oliver, blushing bright red.

Then, at Broomstick Training, Bully Bogeywort knocked Oliver off his broomstick. He landed in the frog pond with an enormous SP-LASH!

"Croak!" burped a frog, bouncing out of his cloak pocket.

"Rats," muttered Oliver, trying to give Bully Bogeywort the evil eye.

The last straw came at lunchtime. When Oliver opened his lunch box, he realized he'd picked up his dad's lunch by mistake. Instead of his favourite bat and lettuce sandwiches, he had his dad's slug and pickle roll. And instead of his usual mould-apple, Oliver had his dad's bunch of worm-berries. Oliver didn't like pickle. And he *hated* worm-berries.

After lunch, Oliver was just about to go outside to play skull football with Jake, when Mrs. MacLizard appeared in the canteen and rapped on one of the tables with a long black fingernail. *Tap, tap, tap.*

"Quiet, please," she said.

The room fell silent. Mrs. MacLizard was usually smiling and jolly. Everyone wondered why she looked so serious today.

"Oliver Moon. A word in my office, please," was all she said.

There was a gasp. GASP!

There was an "Ooh". OOH!

Then there was the rustle of cloaks as every single witch and wizard in the room turned to stare at Oliver.

"Oliver's in trouble, Oliver's in trouble," Bully Bogeywort leered nastily.

Oliver gave him his best eyeball-fizzling look. Then he slowly got to his feet and followed Mrs. MacLizard's long swishing cloak down the corridor.

Was he in trouble? he wondered. Had Mrs. MacLizard heard that he had turned Mr. Goosepimple into a donkey by mistake?

Oliver bit his lip. It *had* been a mistake, though. He hadn't done it on purpose!

They had reached Mrs. MacLizard's office. The heavy wooden door swung open with a *cre-e-eak!*

Oliver felt as if the slug he'd eaten was still wriggling around inside his tummy. Or was that just nerves? He gulped. He'd never been called to the head teacher's office before. He must be in really BIG trouble!

Chapter Three

"Sit," Mrs. MacLizard told him.

His knees knocking, Oliver sat down and looked around.

The walls were lined with jars and bottles. Dead snakes floated in one jar of pink liquid. Beetles crawled around in another. Yellow-toothed rats squeaked and scampered in a huge cage under the window.

"CARK!" croaked a raven, landing on Mrs. MacLizard's left shoulder.

Oliver jumped.

Mrs. MacLizard smiled. "Don't mind him," she said, patting the raven's glossy wing. "He's just nosey. Aren't you, my little feather-flap?"

Then she peered at Oliver's pale face.
"Goodness, you look scared to death!"
she cried. "Don't worry – nothing's wrong.
In fact, quite the opposite!"

A big breath of relief rushed out of
Oliver. "The opposite?" he echoed.

Mrs. MacLizard rummaged in a tray of
papers on her desk. "Where did I put it?"
she muttered. "Ahh! Here."

She passed Oliver a letter that had a picture of a black hat at the top of it. "You'll have to read it," she declared. "I've no *idea* where my glasses are."

Oliver took the letter. It was from *The Pointy Hat*, a spellcraft magazine. The letter said:

Dear Mrs. MacLizard,

Thank you for nominating some of your pupils for the Young Wizard Of The Year award. We are delighted to inform you that two of them have made it onto our shortlist. Their names are Oliver Moon and

Oliver stopped reading and blinked. "Me?" he asked. "Shortlisted for Young Wizard Of The Year?" Wow! Oliver hadn't felt so excited since the day he'd waved his first beginner's wand.

Mrs. MacLizard's beam was so wide that Oliver could see all of her rotten black teeth. "Yes, you," she said. "You and Merlin Spoonbender. It's very exciting. He's already gone into the potions lab to start practising."

Oliver's excitement faded a little. "Merlin Spoonbender?" he repeated. He was up against Merlin Spoonbender, head wizard at school, and captain of the broomstick racing team? Merlin Spoonbender who'd won the school prize year after year for his perfect potions?

Mrs. MacLizard nodded happily. "And there are three wizards from Abracadabra Academy, too," she went on. "But you're the youngest to be chosen for the shortlist, Oliver. It's a real honour, you know!"

Oliver turned back to the letter, his mind in a whirl.

In order to make a final decision, our team of judges will be travelling the country to meet all the young wizards and their families.

Oliver stopped. Hang on. What was that last bit?

our team of judges will be travelling the country to meet all the young wizards and their families.

Their families? The judges wanted to meet his family?

"That's right," Mrs. MacLizard said, as if she was reading Oliver's thoughts. "They always meet the family. Check the young wizard comes from good magical stock. They look around the house, too. It's very important that the Young Wizard Of The Year lives the proper wizarding lifestyle."

"Oh," said Oliver miserably. Right. So not only was he up against Merlin Spoonbender and three other wizards, but the judges were going to meet his mum and dad, too. Good magical stock? A proper wizarding lifestyle? Hardly.

Oliver's head drooped. He was doomed.

Surely he was out of the running already!

"You'll have to perform a short test of your spells, potions and broomsticking abilities — but I'm sure you'll have no trouble with that," Mrs. MacLizard went on. She squinted at Oliver's face. "Everything all right?" she asked.

"Yes," Oliver fibbed. Really, though, he felt almost as miserable as he had done the day Mum had hoovered up his mould collection by mistake.

"Good," said Mrs. MacLizard. She was smiling so widely now that one of her warts *burst* and splattered Oliver in the face. "Best of luck, then!" she said cheerily.

Oliver wiped the yellow wart-goo out of his eyes with his cloak sleeve.

"Th-thank you," he said, trying not to
sigh. He knew it was going to take more
than just luck for him to become the
Young Wizard Of The Year. It was going
to take a miracle!

Chapter Four

That afternoon, when Oliver came home from school, he tried to see the Moon house through the judges' eyes.

Front garden full of nettles and poisonous snakes. That was a good start.

Poison ivy growing over the front door. Very tasteful.

A doorbell that cackled horribly at you when you pressed it. A nice, homely touch.

So far, so magically good. It was only
once the judges stepped inside the house,
they would start to have doubts.

What was that smell in the air? they
would think. *Air freshener? YUCK!*

What was that on the cloak rack? *A leather jacket? And a football scarf? Oh dear!*

And who was that, wearing a pink T-shirt and spotless white shorts, cleaning away the cobwebs in the sitting room? Oliver's mother? Oliver's *mother*?

No pointy hat, no cloak? Clean hair and pink nail varnish? Oh dear. What a state she looked!

Over in the kitchen...who was that, waiting for his pig-trotter pies to cook in the microwave? Oliver's *father*? No!

But where were *his* hat and cloak? And the kitchen spell books? Why was the cauldron so dusty? And what on earth was that on Mr. Moon's head? Surely it wasn't... Tell us it wasn't...

Was that really a *baseball cap*?

Oliver closed his eyes and shuddered. He could already imagine the pitying looks the judges would give him. And wait until they saw the Witch Baby's bedroom that Mum had just wallpapered in lilac and pink! He would never win the contest. No way. It was all going to be so embarrassing!

Oliver opened his eyes suddenly as a thought struck him. He still had four whole days before the judges' visit, didn't he? And maybe – just maybe – he could change things around a little before then…

Oliver went to find his parents. There was no time to lose!

*

The following Saturday, Oliver woke up
feeling wibbly with nerves. He swung his
legs out of his spiderweb hammock, and
took three deep breaths. Today was the
day the judges were coming!

Oliver put on his best purple cloak with
the shiniest moons and stars on it. He
stuck on eight fake beard bristles, and

pulled on his pointiest hat. Then he stared
at his reflection. He looked... He looked...

"Oh dear," the mirror clucked. "Looking
a tad tired there, Oliver, old boy."

"Yucky Ollie!" chirruped the Witch
Baby rather more rudely.

Oliver sighed. The mirror wasn't wrong.
Neither was his sister. And that was
hardly surprising.

Oliver had just had the longest week of his life. He had worked his holey black socks off, trying to turn the house into a fitting place for a Young Wizard Of The Year to live.

He had brought in an emergency team of spiders to spin thick, white webs in each room.

He had sprayed Stinkifier everywhere to get rid of all the clean smells.

He had dusted the cauldron and filled
it with rotten vegetables and dead things,
ready to cook for the judges' lunch.

He had planted Quick-Gro mould in
the carpets and watered it every day.

He had put all the spell books back on
the shelves.

He had hung up the cloaks in the
hall. And he had lined up all the
broomsticks next to them.

The Moon house was looking
marvellously magical again, but that
had only been part of the problem. Oliver
had also needed to make Mum, Dad and
the Witch Baby look more magical, too.
That had been ten times harder.

First, Oliver had hidden all their colourful clothes and Dad's awful baseball cap in a chest, and magicked the lock so that only he could open it. Cloaks and pointy hats were to be worn at all times. The Witch Baby was too young to wear a pointy hat, but Oliver threw away her pink knitted bonnet and found a friendly toad for her to wear instead.

The Witch Baby was very keen on her toad hat. She liked it almost as much as wearing her slug porridge.

Next, Oliver had made his dad park the car far away from the Moons' house. All travelling had to be done on broomsticks, however cold it was.

Then, Oliver had hidden Dad's microwave with an invisibility spell. All cooking was to be done in the cauldron.

Finally, he had replaced all the shampoo, bubble bath and toothpaste with snail-slime hair greaser, skunk-whiff bath potion, and teeth-rotter paste.

Oliver had also rehearsed a few questions that the judges might have for his parents. His mum and dad were keen to help – but they weren't very good at remembering the right answers.

Over breakfast, Oliver decided to run through what he'd taught them, one last time.

"So, Mum, when the judges get here, what are you going to say?" Oliver asked.

Oliver's mum thought carefully. "I'll say, 'Come in, take your shoes off. Who wants a nice cup of herbal tea?'"

Oliver spluttered into his beetle-crunch cereal. "No! That was what you *used* to say. Try again!"

Mrs. Moon's forehead wrinkled as she thought. "Hmm. What was it again?" she frowned. Then her eyes lit up. "I'll say, 'Come in, please wipe your muddy feet on the carpet,'" she replied after a few moments.

"Bogey, bogey, bogey," the Witch Baby muttered to her toad hat.

Oliver nodded. "Good work, both of you," he said. "Dad?"

Mr. Moon munched his bat-wing toast thoughtfully. "Er…I'm going to say, 'Hello there! Who would like a nice jam crumpet?'" he tried.

Oliver put his head in his hands. "No, Dad!" he groaned. "Think!"

"Smelly jelly, smelly jelly," the Witch Baby chanted, smearing porridge dreamily into her eyebrows.

"Better," Oliver said encouragingly. "Dad?"

Mr. Moon scratched his head and knocked his pointy hat onto the floor. Then he brightened. "I'll say, 'Who

would like some cockroach cake?'" he
cried, looking pleased with himself.

"Yes," Oliver said in relief. "Please try
to get it right!"

Just then, someone rang the doorbell
and a cackle echoed around the house.

AH-HA-HA-HA-HA-HA!

"That's a nice, homely touch," the Moons heard someone say outside the front door.

Oliver's heart skipped a beat. The judges had arrived!

Chapter
Five

When Oliver opened the front door, there were three judges outside.

The first judge was fat and whiskery, with the longest, whitest beard Oliver had ever seen. He had hairy nostrils and black teeth. "I'm Hogbreath Hardgrip," he said, and he squeezed Oliver's hand so tightly that his knuckles cracked.

The second judge was tall and skinny. She had long, silver hair and half-moon spectacles. "I'm Nettle Poisonpetal," she said, with a gentle smile.

The third judge had one green eye and one blue eye. She had more wrinkles than Oliver could count, and seven bony fingers on each hand. She had a few wisps of fluffy white hair, but apart from that she was as bald as an ostrich egg. "I'm the Ancient One," she said.

Suddenly, Oliver was hit by nerves. They were here, at his house, to see him, to judge if he was good enough to be Young Wizard Of The Year! How scary could you get?

Then he heard a voice from somewhere

around his ankles. "Wipe feet!" ordered
the Witch Baby bossily.

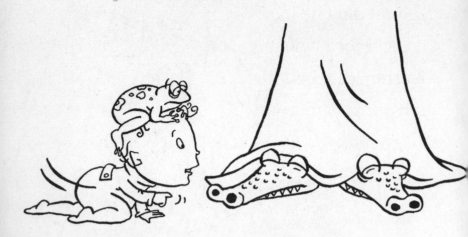

Oliver's mum cleared her throat
hurriedly. "Yes, just what I was about to
say. Er… Do come in – please wipe your
muddy feet on the carpet!"

Oliver winked down at the Witch
Baby, who was waving a chubby hand at
the judges. "Smelly jelly," she said in a
friendly manner.

Mr. Moon beamed. "That reminds me. Would anyone like a cockroach cake? Freshly killed and roasted this morning!"

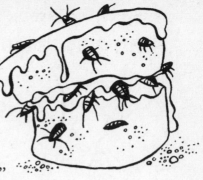

"Sounds *frightfully* good," cackled the Ancient One, daintily wiping her crocodile shoes all over the carpet.

Oliver jumped as one of the crocodile's eyes suddenly opened and gave him a slow, yellow wink. "Um… Come through to the kitchen," he managed to say, feeling dazed.

"What a marvellously magical room," Hogbreath Hardgrip said, as he stepped through the slime puddles on the kitchen floor.

"Super cauldron," Nettle Poisonpetal
added. "Is it a Slo-Bubble?"

"That's right," Oliver heard Dad
saying. "We do all our cooking in it."
He pulled his shoulders up proudly.
"We're very traditional when it comes to

cooking, aren't we, son?" He winked
across the room at him. "In fact, Oliver's
got some lunch on the go at the moment.
Dead-thing casserole, I believe."

"Oh, goody," the Ancient One croaked.
"My favourite."

"Poo," agreed the Witch Baby, feeding
a dead rat to the Ancient One's crocodile
shoes.

Oliver took a deep breath, praying his
family could keep up the good work.
"Would you like to see the rest of our
home?" he asked politely.

*

"Smashing collection of spell books," Hogbreath Hardgrip said approvingly a few minutes later, as they strolled around the house. "Oliver's lucky to have such educated parents."

"We do our best," Mrs. Moon told him, batting her eyelashes.

"I saw the broomsticks in the hall," Nettle Poisonpetal said. "A good range you've got there."

"There's nothing better than a family broomsticking trip out," Mr. Moon smiled.

"Car," the Witch Baby said loudly, and Oliver shot her an agonized look.

"Car BAD," the Witch Baby added, and burped, with a toothy grin.

"Yes, very bad," Mrs. Moon said quickly. "I've never understood why people drive around in those contraptions. Apart from the stereos, of course... Wonderful inventions," she said, looking rather dreamy.

Oliver trod hard on his mum's foot.

"Ouch!" she squeaked.

"Or so we've heard, anyway," Mr. Moon put in hastily. "Isn't that right, my little cockroach? Now. Shall we eat?"

*

"Delicious casserole, sonny," the Ancient One said to Oliver, after she'd gobbled up a huge plateful. "Is it an old family recipe?"

"It's one that Dad and I invented together," Oliver fibbed, crossing his fingers under the table. He didn't dare look his dad in the eye.

"Marvellous. That's what we like to see – older wizards passing on their wisdom to the younger generation," the Ancient One said. She belched so loudly the whole table shook, and green vapours filled the room.

"Yum," the Witch Baby commented

gleefully, trying to catch them in a podgy fist.

Hogbreath checked his watch. "We'd better move on to the magic tests, now, Oliver," he said. "Spells first, then potions."

"Of course," Oliver replied, feeling nervous. He'd been so busy sorting out his house and parents, he'd hardly had any time to practise for the magic tests.

"Now then," Nettle said. "Let's see if you know the Transforma spell well enough to turn me into a sausage sandwich."

Oliver almost groaned out loud as he took up his wand. The Transforma spell? The very spell he'd got wrong at school on Monday!

"Porkus…" Oliver began slowly, "donkus…butty…tom–" Then he stopped suddenly. Hang on. That's what he'd said last time, when he'd turned Mr. Goosepimple into a donkey. He couldn't do the same thing again!

Oliver cast his eyes around the kitchen, desperately trying to remember what Mr. Goosepimple had said, apart from "Hee-haw". Then he noticed that the crocodile on the Ancient One's shoe was

licking its lips in a meaningful way.

Oliver raised his wand again, suddenly feeling confident. "Porkus…DROOLUS… butty…tommy-kay!" he chanted, waving his wand over Nettle.

There was a round of applause as a delicious-looking sausage sandwich appeared on the table.

"Oooh!" squeaked the Witch Baby, stretching out an eager hand for it.

"Spell – reverse! Before this gets worse!" Oliver chanted hurriedly. He really didn't want his sister to *eat* the *judge*! He waved his wand quickly – but a little too quickly. Magic dust flew everywhere around the kitchen and then, to Oliver's horror, there was an unmistakable sound. PING!

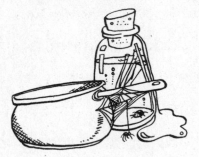

Chapter Six

Oliver could hardly bear to look. Behind the judges' backs, a familiar white object had just appeared. His spell-reverse command had reversed the invisibility spell that he had put on the microwave, as well as the Transforma spell. If any of the judges saw the Moons' microwave, he'd be out of the competition. Everybody knew that real wizards didn't use microwaves!

Hogbreath Hardgrip frowned and cocked his head. "Did somebody say something?" he asked.

"It sounded like a PING!" Nettle said, wiping tomato sauce out of her hair as she reappeared in the kitchen.

"A PING?" the Ancient One echoed, looking puzzled. "Or a PONG?"

"Is it the potions test next?" Oliver asked quickly, trying to distract them.

PING!

"There it goes again," Nettle said. Then, to Oliver's horror, she turned around. Her eyes fell upon the microwave, and there was a terrible silence. "Is that what I think it is?" she asked in a cold voice.

Oliver quaked. "Um…" he stammered. However was he going to explain *this*? "No," he said, racking his brains. "Well, yes. But we use it as a… As a potion-prep machine."

"A *what*?" Hogbreath said, raising a bushy eyebrow.

"A p…p…" Oliver stuttered. It was difficult to speak with Hogbreath's disbelieving gaze upon him.

"A potion-prep machine," Oliver's dad interrupted breezily. "Didn't you notice it earlier? It's our pride and joy, isn't it,

Ol?" he went on. "You can use it for warming all sorts of things – bats, toads, herbs... It's perfect for potion preparation. Every modern wizard should have one!"

There was a silence around the table as the judges looked at one another. Oliver shot his dad a thankful look.

"What a marvellous idea!" the Ancient One croaked, a smile lighting up her wrinkles. "Ingenious, Mr. Moon!"

"Oh, don't praise me, it was Oliver who thought of it," Mr. Moon said, putting a proud arm around his son. "Bringing magic into the twenty-first century, that's Oliver's attitude."

Oliver felt his heart slowing from its rapid thump. He'd got away with it! He'd actually...

"I look forward to seeing you use it for the potions test," the Ancient One said at that moment. "Shall we begin?"

Oliver's smile froze on his face. His mouth felt dry. He *hadn't* got away with it, after all. He'd never used Dad's stupid microwave in his life! "Of course," he said, swallowing hard. "What would you like me to make?"

"A pimplesqueeze potion, please," Hogbreath Hardgrip replied. He twiddled a hairy pimple on his left cheek. "Let's see if you can get this beauty to blow!"

Oliver took a deep breath. The pimplesqueeze potion was very difficult to make. If it was prepared correctly, it could blow the pimples off whoever drank it. But if the potion *wasn't* made correctly, then it tended to blow off beards, eyelashes and eyebrows as well. And Oliver knew that a hair explosion in his kitchen would not go down at all well with the judges!

With shaking fingers,
Oliver selected
his ingredients.
Lizard legs – three.

 Raven feathers – two.
Crumbled caterpillar
eggs – one
teaspoonful. Ripe
prickleberries – five…ahh.

As Oliver opened the fridge door to get
out the prickleberries, he realized with a
gulp that they were
right at the back by
the ice compartment
– and had frozen
into a solid lump!

"PING!" sang the
Witch Baby cheerily.

Oliver gazed up at the microwave hopefully. Could it really help him? He was going to have to try.

"Obviously, frozen prickleberries will spoil the potion," Oliver declared, trying to sound as if he knew all about such things. "But if I warm them up in the microwave for about…um…five minutes," he said, guessing wildly, "then…"

"*Seconds…*" his dad mouthed.

"Five seconds, I mean," Oliver said, walking quickly to the microwave so that the judges couldn't see his blushes, "then it should work perfectly."

Oliver put the iced berries into the microwave, then shut the door. *Now what?* he wondered. How did you start this stupid machine anyway?

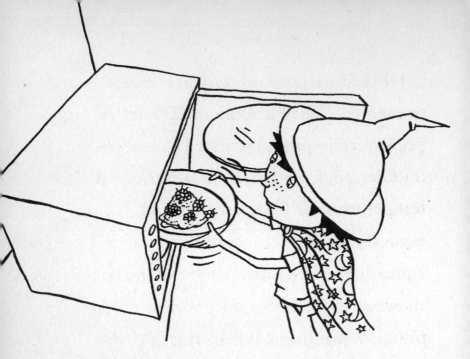

He pressed the "5" button hopefully.
Nothing happened.

"Of course, it sometimes takes a
second or two to START," his dad said
meaningfully.

Oliver's eyes fell upon a button marked
"START", and he jabbed it quickly.
Whirr... went the microwave. *Whirr...*
Whirr... PING!

His heart thudding, Oliver cautiously opened the microwave door. The prickleberries had separated from one another, and were just the right temperature. It had worked! It had actually worked!

"And now you can see," he said, showing the judges, "that these prickleberries are perfect for a potion!"

"Most impressive," Hogbreath said, nodding approvingly.

"Excellent!" Nettle agreed.

"I must get one of those machines myself," the Ancient One said thoughtfully.

Oliver got to work with his potion. He poured all the ingredients into a beaker and heated it over the cauldron.

Then he gave it three stirs, tapped it with his wand and muttered, "Pimplesqueeze, pimplesqueeze, pimplesqueeze," adding in a very quiet voice, "Please."

The potion shimmered with strange purple and silver swirls. It was ready!

Oliver poured it into a goblet and
passed it to Hogbreath Hardgrip.

Hogbreath peered into the potion and
sniffed it. Then he gulped it down.

Oliver held his breath. What was going
to happen? Would his pimplesqueeze
potion pass the test?

Chapter Seven

Nothing happened for a few moments.
Then suddenly the hairy pimple on
Hogbreath's cheek glowed a luminous
yellow – and erupted. Sticky pimple-goo
spurted onto the table with a loud
splatter.

Oliver was still holding his breath, half
expecting Hogbreath's eyelashes and

beard to follow but they stayed firmly on his face. He'd done it!

Hogbreath let out a loud belch. "Splendid," he told Oliver, smiling.

The Witch Baby threw her toad hat in the air, and it landed with a startled croak on the table. "Good, Oliver!" she cheered.

Oliver couldn't help grinning in sheer relief. Potion panic over!

The rest of the judges' visit went smoothly. Okay, so there was that awful moment in the broomstick-flying test when he almost crashed into the tanglebranch tree – but on the whole, he did well. And thank goodness the visit had ended!

"Thank you," Hogbreath said, at the end. "We've seen all five shortlisted wizards now, so we will leave you while we make our decision."

"We'll send for you when we're about to announce the results," Nettle added. Then she waved her wand, and the three judges vanished.

"Well done, Oliver," his mum said, hugging him tightly. "You were brilliant!"

"Thanks, Mum, thanks, Dad," Oliver replied. "You were both great, too. Fingers crossed that—"

But before he could finish his sentence, a silvery trail of sparkling magic dust came snaking through the air towards the Moon family.

"That was quick," Mr. Moon gaped. "The judges must have picked a winner already!"

The silvery trail wrapped itself around them all, and the garden blurred before Oliver's eyes. He felt himself hurtling through the air – before landing with a bump in a grand hall. He looked around to see the four other shortlisted wizards and their families bumping down around him. They were all on a big stage, in front of an audience, who were clapping each arrival.

Oliver glanced over at the other four wizards. None of them looked as nervous as *he* was feeling. In fact, all four of them were smiling confidently. They all must have done really, really well!

The three judges appeared onstage in a
puff of silvery smoke, and silence fell.

Nettle smiled at the audience. "I'm
delighted to announce that all three of us
were in agreement as to the winner of this

year's Young Wizard Of The Year contest," she said. "And that winner is...Merlin Spoonbender!"

Oliver's shoulders drooped. He should have known. How could he ever have hoped to beat Merlin?

Everybody clapped as Merlin went up to collect his trophy.

Mrs. Moon put her arm around Oliver. "Never mind," she said, kissing the top of his head. "We're very proud of you."

"Manky Merlin," the Witch Baby muttered crossly, sticking her tongue out at him.

"Just one more thing," Nettle went on, once the applause had died down. "We have decided to award an extra prize this year, to the wizard who showed the most promise for the future. For bringing a modern touch to wizardry with his...er...potion-prep machine, the prize goes to...Oliver Moon!"

Lots of exciting things happened after that. Oliver was given a gold award in the shape of a broomstick, and photographers from *The Pointy Hat*, *Wizarding Weekly* and *Practical Potioncraft* all took photos of him. A wizard from the local TV station even flew by to film Oliver and Merlin for the evening news.

Then, just as suddenly as it had started, it was all over again and they were transported back home. Time to get back to normal.

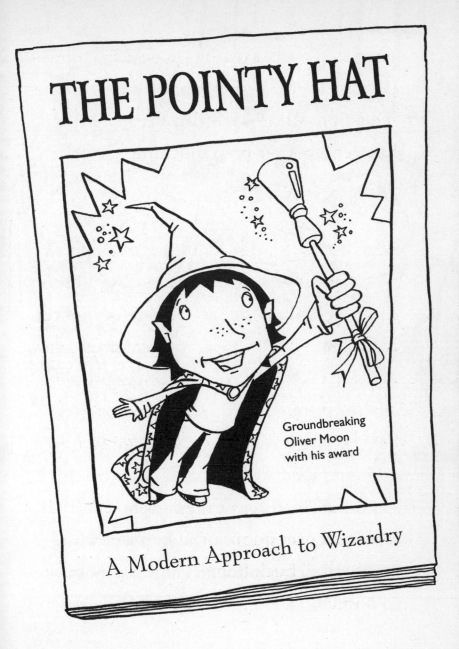

THE POINTY HAT

Groundbreaking
Oliver Moon
with his award

A Modern Approach to Wizardry

"I couldn't have done it without you,
Mum and Dad," Oliver said happily, the
next day. The three of them were
drinking worm juice in the kitchen, while
the Witch Baby munched cockroaches in
her high chair. He grinned at them. "So

you don't have to wear your cloaks and hats any more, if you don't want to. And you can bring the car back again, Dad."

Oliver's mum and dad looked at each other.

"Well..." Oliver's mum said.

"Actually..." Oliver's dad started.

They paused. "To tell the truth, I'm rather enjoying being back on the broomstick," Mrs. Moon said, fiddling with her spider earrings. "I'd forgotten how much fun seagull racing is. The wind rushing through your hair. Surfing the clouds..."

"Wheeee!" put in the Witch Baby.

Oliver's eyes boggled in surprise. "Oh," he said. "Great!"

"And actually, I'd forgotten just how comfortable a cloak is," Oliver's dad confessed. "Those trousers...well, they were a bit on the tight side to be honest. And it *is* nice to swish my cloak again."

"SWISH!" shouted the Witch Baby.

Oliver's eyes boggled even more. "Right," he said. "That's brilliant! So you're going to be a good old-fashioned witch and wizard from now on, are you?"

There was a pause.

And then there was a PING!

Oliver's dad got up. "Almost," he grinned. "Microwaved slugs on toast for tea all right with everyone?"

The End

Don't miss Oliver's fab website,
where you can find lots of fun, free stuff.
Log on now...

www.olivermoon.co.uk

Oliver Moon
Junior Wizard

Collect all of Oliver Moon's magical adventures!

All books are priced at £3.99